Race
Further
with
Reading

THE TERRIFYING TEACHER

By Claire O'Brien

Illustrated by Santy Gutierrez

W
FRANKLIN WATTS
LONDON•SYDNEY

CHAPTER ONE
Moon Day

There is something different about
our new teacher, Mr Bloodaxe.

He isn't like Miss Pomegranate, who wears flowers in her hair and plays the piano. He isn't like Mr Mustard, who wears sports kit and has a big, smooth chin, and he isn't like Mrs Snapper, the headteacher, who wears high heels and has a smile like a shark.

Mr Bloodaxe is about seven feet tall.
His hair is long and fair, and some of
it is plaited. His HUGE beard is as red
as a bonfire and he wears a tunic with
a belt.

This morning, he arrived at school in a
Viking longboat. I saw him rowing it up
the canal.

When he took the register Mr Bloodaxe
shouted with a voice like THUNDER. He
called Matthew's name and Matthew, who
is cheeky, replied, "Here I am, Goldilocks."
It was a BIG mistake to call Mr Bloodaxe
Goldilocks ...

... because Matthew spent the whole
morning dangling out of the window by his
ankles. It was lucky that our classroom isn't
on the top floor because Matthew is scared
of heights.

While Matthew was dangling, the rest of us had to do Viking exercises.

"You must all learn to be TOUGH," said Mr Bloodaxe. "Vikings are TOUGH and STRONG."

We had to lift boulders and try to throw them. Betty was brilliant at this, but she dropped a boulder on Alison's toe and poor Alison had to go to hospital.

Next, we had to practise screaming at our enemies.

"Pull a scary face," Mr Bloodaxe told us, "Like THIS." His face was so scary that Jasmine cried.

"Now, run across the field screaming as loudly as you can," Mr Bloodaxe told us. This was great fun but Mrs Snapper soon complained about the noise.

"We will do wrestling instead," said Mr
Bloodaxe. I had to wrestle with Betty's twin
brother, Ben. He is much stronger than me
so he just sat on me and I couldn't move.
"This isn't a fair fight," I told Mr Bloodaxe.
Vikings aren't FAIR," Mr Bloodaxe yelled.
"They are TOUGH and MEAN."

At last it was story time and we could sit down quietly, but Mr Bloodaxe's stories were VERY gruesome. Betty and Ben loved them but Tom was scared and Alice felt sick. "May I go and draw a picture of a fairy instead?" she asked.

"Vikings don't believe in fairies!" yelled Mr Bloodaxe. "We believe in TROLLS!"

There was a THUMP THUMP sound from under the floorboards.

"Don't upset my troll," Mr Bloodaxe warned us. "Vikings are tough but trolls are TOUGHER."

THUMP

THUMP

CHAPTER TWO
Tyr's Day

The next day Mr Bloodaxe brought a heavy sword and a round wooden shield with him. He also brought two ENORMOUS ravens. Their eyes were black and shiny and their feathers were as dark as coal.

"These are Hugin and Mugin," he told us. "They tell me everything and they will be watching you."

That morning we learned how to scrape reindeer skins clean with bits of bone. This was the most disgusting thing I have ever done. We had to work really hard while Mr Bloodaxe practised whacking chairs in half with his sword.

"Make sure you scrape all the bits of dead reindeer off," Mr Bloodaxe ordered. "Those skins will keep us warm on our sea voyage."

Later, some of us had to paint his longboat with sticky tar.

"The tar will keep the sea water out," he told us. "Put plenty on." Polly got tar stuck in her pigtails so Mr Bloodaxe gave her a haircut with his sword. She was very upset.

After lunch, Mr Bloodaxe showed us how to take the insides out of dead fish and smoke them over a fire. This was even worse than scraping reindeer skins. Fish guts are extra whiffy, and the smoke from the fire made us cough.

"Delicious herring for our sea voyage," said Mr Bloodaxe. "Yummy!"

Ben and Betty didn't seem to mind the stink. They enjoyed feeding fish guts to the ravens.

At snack time we had dried polar bear meat.
Alastair told Mr Bloodaxe that he was a
vegetarian and couldn't possibly eat polar
bear. Mr Bloodaxe just laughed in a scary
way and stuck Alastair's veggie banger
sandwich on a spike outside the school gate.

"Let that be a warning to our enemies," he told us. Then he made Alastair sit in the book corner, but he took all of the books away! Alastair loves reading so this was like a TERRIBLE TORTURE for him.

"He'll die of boredom without a book to read," Sajid whispered to me. I nodded. I really wanted to help Alastair, but was I brave enough?

At lunchtime Mr Bloodaxe had a nap and snored like a walrus. Sajid and I crept inside to try and pass Alastair a book to read and some carrots to eat. We were nearly there when we heard the THUMP THUMP sound from under the floorboards again. We froze. There was definitely something very big under our classroom.

THUMP

Then we saw the ravens watching us. They
SQUAWKED and Mr Bloodaxe woke up.
"What's going on!" he roared.
"Quick, hide behind the coats," said Sajid.
Poor Alastair was stuck in the book corner
for the next three days.

CHAPTER THREE
Odin's Day

Mr Bloodaxe showed us an old map.

"These are the best places for Vikings to invade," he told us. He explained that invading somewhere means killing people in horrible ways, taking slaves, stealing food and sheep, and burning villages.

Betty and Ben wanted to do a real invasion but the rest of us weren't so sure.

"It sounds quite dangerous," said Jessica.

"Yes," agreed Sajid, "and it's better to make friends with people from other countries rather than chop them up."

Mr Bloodaxe went purple and steam came out of his hairy nostrils.

"Vikings don't CARE about danger," he roared. "We don't CARE about making friends. We want to be rich and powerful."

After that, he made the whole class row
his longboat up and down the canal for
HOURS.

"You must get stronger and TOUGHER!"
he shouted. "You must be skilled with oar,
sword and axe to be a Viking."

I decided that I would have to be brave
and say something.

"Some of us don't really want to be Vikings,
sir," I said. "I would much rather be a vet."

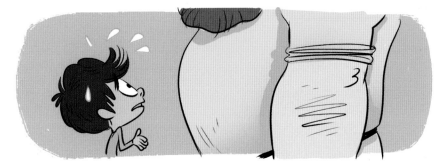

Mr Bloodaxe frowned at me very deeply.

"Any more talk about not wanting to be a
Viking and you'll be troll food," he growled.

"There isn't really a troll, sir." I said. "We
all know that." I shouldn't have said that
because Mr Bloodaxe just laughed his scary
laugh and said, "You'll soon see."

At home time things seemed to get better. Mr Bloodaxe said, "Bring your favourite toy to school tomorrow."

"That's nice," said Alice. "Perhaps he's just a big softy underneath."

We were all looking forward to sharing our toys, but Mr Bloodaxe had a very different plan.

CHAPTER FOUR
Thor's Day

My favourite toy is my big soft dinosaur, so I took him to school the next day. Alice brought her collection of fairies. Matthew brought his toy giraffes. Sajid brought his bulldozer.

Ben and Betty brought a big rhinoceros.
Jessica had a whole family of fluffy rabbit
toys with her and Polly carried her box of
squeezy paint tubes.

We were showing each other our favourite things when Mr Bloodaxe walked in with a raven on each shoulder. He wore a chain mail vest and carried his sword and spear.

He put down his weapons and took the toys.
"Vikings do not PLAY with toys. Your toys
will be traded for gold and slaves."
We all GASPED. He couldn't possibly mean
it! Could he? We didn't want to trade our
favourite toys for ANYTHING.

All morning, Mr Bloodaxe made us do target practice with swords and spears. He used scarecrows as targets.

"Anyone who won't join in will be fed to the troll," Mr Bloodaxe warned us. We didn't dare refuse, just in case there really was a troll.

He marched up and down behind us.
"Mash them! Spear them! Chop them!" he
shouted. Betty and Ben loved it but the rest
of us thought it was a bit silly. Afterwards,
the playground was a terrible mess. There
were bits of scarecrow all over the place.

Later, we had salted seal blubber for snacks. I thought I heard the troll growling under the floorboards again, but perhaps it was just my tummy complaining – seal blubber is not easy to digest.

I managed to sneak a book and a chocolate bar to Alastair before home time and whisper, "Don't worry, Alastair. We'll think of something."

CHAPTER FIVE
Freya's Day

On Friday morning Mr Bloodaxe wore all his Viking clothes. His shield was strapped to his back as well as a big axe. It looked very sharp and the edge was still red from chopping something up.

"Today we set sail on our first raid," he told us. "I have decided to invade Iceland."

Ben and Betty were very excited but no one

else wanted to go.

"It's Jason's birthday party this weekend,"

said Jessica. "We don't want to miss it."

"No," Trevor agreed. "Birthday cake tastes

much nicer than polar bear and seal

blubber."

But the ravens stared at us with their sharp, black eyes and CAW CAWED. We heard the THUMP THUMP sound from under the floorboards again and Mr Bloodaxe held up his axe, yelling, "You are ALL Vikings now!"

THUMP

THUMP

We had to pack the longboat with polar bear snacks, salted seal blubber, reindeer skins, smoked herring and cheese.

While we worked hard, Mr Bloodaxe
tried to catch fish in the canal.
"Vikings must be skilled with a fishing rod,
too," he told us. Then he sat very still for a
long, long time. Sajid whispered to me,
"I think he's fallen asleep."

We all crept away but before we got to the school gates there was a terrible ROAR. The classroom windows broke, the door fell off and that's when we saw the TROLL.

It was green and hairy. It had fierce red eyes and big yellow teeth. It had fists like hammers and legs like tree trunks, and it looked VERY ANGRY INDEED.

Mr Bloodaxe woke up suddenly.

"Drat!" he shouted, pulling out his sword and raising his shield. "I forgot to feed him."

"Quick," I whispered to Sajid. "Let's go and get Alastair."

While Mr Bloodaxe fought the troll we ran
inside and rescued Alastair from the book
corner. He looked a bit pale and thin but
he was okay.

"Everybody run to my house!" I shouted.

We all RAN. Even Betty and Ben ran.

Mr Bloodaxe had to face the angry troll

on his own.

He was right when he said that trolls are even tougher than Vikings, because he soon had to run for his longboat.

He jumped aboard with the ravens flapping above him and rowed with all his strength. The troll jumped into the canal and swam after him. And that was the last we saw of Mr Bloodaxe.

School was closed for two whole weeks (hooray!) while the teachers found a new building. Today is our first day back and we have another new teacher. Betty and Ben look quite pleased, but I'm not so sure about Mr Hook.

Franklin Watts
First published in Great Britain in 2016 by
The Watts Publishing Group

Text © Claire O'Brien 2016
Illustrations © Santy Gutierrez 2016

The rights of Claire O'Brien to be
identified as the author and Santy Gutierrez
as the illustrator of this Work have been
asserted in accordance with the Copyright,
Designs and Patents Act, 1988.

Series Editor: Melanie Palmer
Series Advisor: Catherine Glavina
Cover Designer: Cathryn Gilbert
Design Manager: Peter Scoulding

A CIP catalogue record for this book is
available from the British Library.

ISBN 978 1 4451 4999 8 (hbk)
ISBN 978 1 4451 4997 4 (pbk)
ISBN 978 1 4451 4998 1 (library ebook)

Printed in China

Franklin Watts
An imprint of
Hachette Children's Group
Part of The Watts Publishing Group
Carmelite House
50 Victoria Embankment
London EC4Y 0DZ

An Hachette UK Company
www.hachette.co.uk

www.franklinwatts.co.uk